READING Makes You Feel Good

Todd PARR

Megan Tingley Books

LITTLE, BROWN AND COMPANY

New York · Boston

To my Grandma Logan, who introduced me to
GREEN EGGS AND HAM,
I Love you very much,
Todd

ALSO BY TODD PARR:

The Best Friends Book

The Daddy Book

The Family Book

The Feel Good Book

It's Okay to Be Different

The Mommy Book

The Peace Book

For a complete list of titles and more information about
Todd Parr, his Web site address is:

www.toddparr.com

Little, Brown and Company

Time Warner Book Group
1271 Avenue of the Americas, New York, NY 10020
Visit our Web site at www.lb-kids.com

First Edition

Library of Congress Cataloging-in-Publication Data

Parr, Todd.
  Reading makes you feel good / by Todd Parr.—1st ed.
    p. cm.
  "Megan Tingley Books"
  Summary: Describes the characteristics and various advantages of reading.
  ISBN 0-316-16004-0
    [1. Books and Reading—Fiction.] I. Title.
PZ7.P2447Re 2005
[E]—dc22   2004010274

10 9 8 7 6 5 4 3 2 1

TWP

Printed in Singapore

Reading makes you feel good because...

princess or a scary dinosaur

You can learn about

Book reports
Friday.

You can make

a new friend

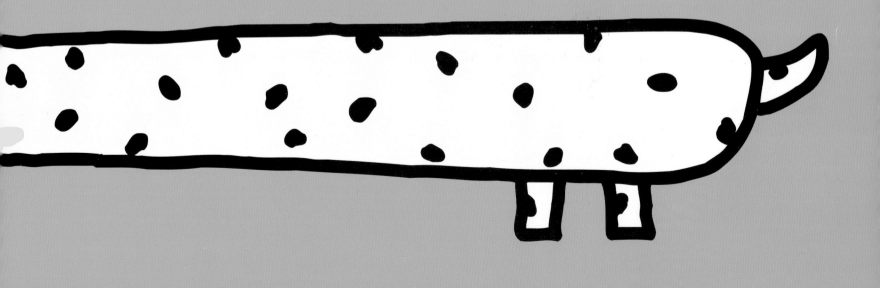

And you can do it anywhere!

to make pizza

animal at the zoo

better when they are sick

faraway places

all by yourself

take care of your pet

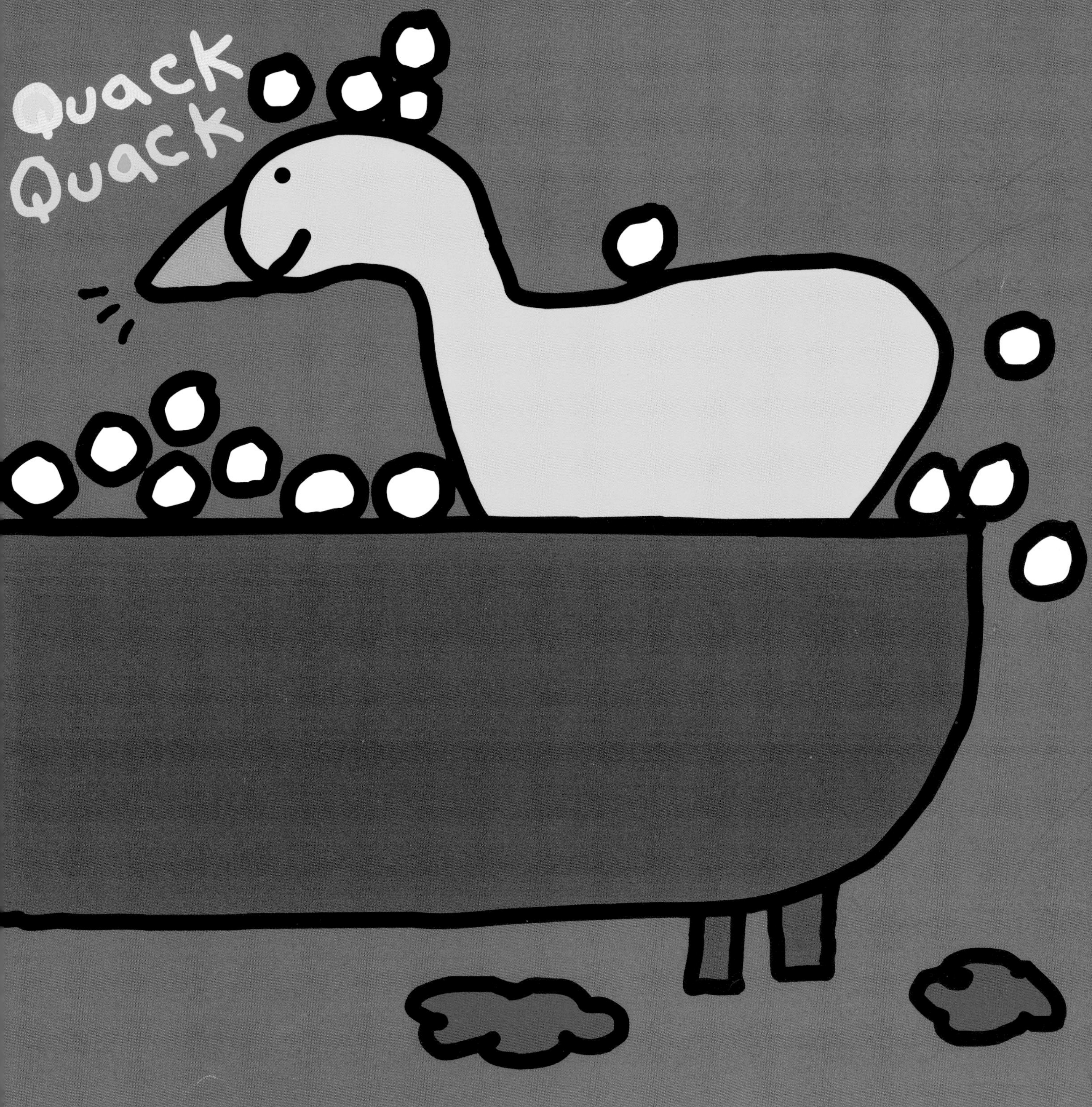

You can share a

book with anyone

And you can

do it anywhere!

Reading is important!
When you read or
someone reads to
you it helps you learn
and discover new things.
Curl up with someone
special and read a book.
You'll feel really good.
Love,
Todd

P.S. See if you can read all the words I put in the pictures!